The Legend of The Grand Canyon

Retold By
Gloria C. Sproul
Pictures by
Michael Meyer

The Legend of the Grand Canyon copyright 2001 by Gloria C. Sproul

ISBN 0-934372-02-0

Mishe Mokwa Publications
602 S. Avenida Del Monte
Tucson, AZ 85748

Mishe Mokwa Publications
P.O.Box 273
Honor, MI 49640

Special Acknowledgements: To my friends, John and Joyce Campsmith who helped me put the pictures on the computer and who believed in the project. To my son in law, Tom Demsky who first put the story on file, and to my daughter, Lisa, and grandson, Ryan, who encouraged and supported me. A word of special thanks to my son, Trip and daughter in law, Betty, who helped me get it together, kept me focused and supported me during my trying moments. Last, but not least, to my old and dear friend, Kathryn, who first said, "You can't afford not to do it."

Printed in Canada
By Friesens

For my parents, Carl and Kate Carlson, who first introduced me to Arizona, and my late husband Merrill, who showed me the beauty and grandeur of the Grand Canyon.

Also, for our children, Trip, Lisa, Dena and Mari and our grandchildren, Lisa, Dustin, Ryan, Christopher, Eric and Kelsey.

Legends are part of the world's literature, composed by many cultures. American Indian legends stand by themselves as part of our first American's history, explaining the reasons for man's existence and for all of nature.

While researching Indian legends surrounding the origin of the Grand Canyon, I discovered this particular version, which is my favorite, and in no way discounts the others. In this legend I have chosen to name the young chief, Comanche, because of the strength and beauty of the name. It in no way refers to the Comanche tribe who originally lived west of the Rocky Mountains. In addition, I have chosen to have this particular tribe live in tipis (tepees) rather then in caves, kivas, pueblos or hogans.

We are the stars which sing,
We sing with our light
We are the birds of fire,
We fly over the sky.
Our light is a voice;
We make a road for the spirits,
For the spirits to pass over...

An Algonquin Poem

Hundreds of years ago in America, long before the white man came to settle, but at a time when the American Indians lived in the deserts, forests, and mountains of what is now known as the United States of America, a brave, young Indian chief who we will call Comanche, lived and ruled his people in the region of land now known as the Southwest.

Comanche lived among his people with his lovely wife, Kio, whose beauty and whose kindness were known throughout the land.

Whenever Comanche would go on hunts he would bring her skins to line their tipi home. And when he climbed the steep mountain walls, and then descended into the deep caves within, he would collect rocks of blue that she would wear around her neck.

Often in the evening, when the moon and stars were high in the sky, Comanche could be heard singing, as he lulled her to sleep.

One day, after Comanche returned from a long hunt with his braves, he found his beloved wife sick with fever. She lay quietly while the medicine man tried to make her well. Only none of the herbs and

medicines would calm her raging fever. The only nourishment she would take, was the water that Comanche put to her lips.

For days, Comanche refused to leave the side of his beloved, yet nothing seemed to help the beautiful maiden. Finally, the day arrived, when she turned her head and would drink no more.

After many moons, Great Spirit took her to the Great Spirit World that knows no end.

For weeks and months, Comanche grieved over the loss of his beautiful wife. He would no longer join his braves on their tribal hunts. He would not guide his people when they came to him for council. He even refused the food his people brought to his table.

All Comanche would do was lie on the forest grass and look into the clouds above.

One day, as Comanche lay grieving, Great Spirit
spoke to him. His voice roared and the branches of the
trees shook around Comanche as he spoke.

"Rise, Comanche, and follow Shadow One who will lead you
to where Kio is resting. There you may see the face of your beloved
once more."

As Great Spirit spoke, Comanche arose as if from a dream. He turned
to the heavens with his head lifted upward.

"Great Spirit, I have heard your voice. Let me stay with Kio forever.
Without her, I have no life and no heart for my people."

Once again the tree branches shook with the thunder of Great Spirit's
voice.

"Follow Shadow One to the Spirit Trail that leads to the Great
Beyond."

Suddenly, a giant shadow appeared before Comanche and beckoned him. And then without hesitation, he began to follow.

For days Comanche struggled along through forests and mountains. Sometimes when the first stars of the evening darkness appeared, he would lay by some water spring and rest. Then Shadow One would fill Comanche with food and energy while he slept.

In the morning, before the first rays of sun began to break, Comanche would rise and follow Shadow One as they journeyed towards the great rocky crevices, which lay ahead.

At last they arrived at some giant mesas where the jagged rocks stood out like piercing arrows. Once again the earth and branches shook with Great Spirit's voice.

"Climb downward. Inside of this mountain rock is the secret Spirit Trail that leads to the Great Beyond. After many moons you will reach the bottom. Then you will journey down the Spirit Trail where you will view Kio at rest."

No sooner had Great Spirit spoken then the rocks split open, forming a gigantic opening in the middle of the mountains. It was the largest crevice he had ever seen and he gazed downward in wonder.

Then Comanche followed Shadow One down sharp and jagged rocks, which tore his flesh. With bleeding feet he sometimes cried out in pain as they went further into the mountain's depths.

After several moons had passed they finally reached the bottom. Ahead of them, stretching on into the distance was a large, wide trail that seemed to have no end. As Comanche looked upward all he saw were the high walls of rocks that seemed to meet the sky.

Then, without warning, Shadow One disappeared, leaving Comanche alone. He stood there for a while, looking around him. As he began to walk down the trail he suddenly turned his head and raised his eyes to the other side of the canyon. Far up above the peaks, as if in a cloud, appeared the face of his beloved Kio.

She was smiling and waving to him and her hands
went to her lips as she beckoned him to follow.

Comanche began to run towards the cloudy mist where Kio stood
smiling and waving.

Then once again, the earth began to roar and the wind blew, and even the pebbles and sand blew around his feet as the voice of Great Spirit spoke.

"GO HOME COMANCHE. Your people need you. You cannot stay or come back until your tasks on earth are finished. Only then, can you join your beloved in the Great Spirit World that knows no end."

With those words, his beloved Kio disappeared. And then, Comanche felt a trickle of water beneath his feet. As he started to run the water became deeper, so up he climbed to the safety of the rocks.

Then, without warning, a loud roar filled the earth, and a rush of water came through the canyon walls, covering the Spirit Trail forever and forming a giant, swirling river for as far as Comanche could see.

He stood and watched, as the water became deeper and deeper and deeper. He waited and watched as the Spirit Trail completely disappeared and the evening stars and moon came out, casting shadows on the river below.

Then he waited and watched the clouds above for one more glimpse of his beloved Kio. Only alas, she could no longer be seen.

Then sadly, the young chief turned his head, and not looking back, he slowly began his long climb home, knowing in his heart that someday he would see his beloved again.

Today in America, in the region of land in Arizona now known as the Grand Canyon, you can still see the winding river that covers the Spirit Trail.

And if you look closely, you might just see the young chief, Comanche, and his beautiful wife, Kio, together somewhere inside the misty clouds.

His spirit finds its way into the spirit world,
lifted on the wind above the grandeur and
beauty of the earth

Yellow Wolf (Kiowa, 1920)

Michael Meyer has been painting most of his life, with his earliest projects being the walls of his parent's home. A native of Traverse City, Michigan, Michael is currently working towards his B.F.A. in Visual Communication at Kendall College of Art and Design in Grand Rapids, Michigan. He presently holds degrees from two other schools.

Over three years of research and time went into the project squeezed in between work and studies. This is Michael's first book, but not his last. He has one son.

Gloria Carlson Sproul, a native of Frankfort, Michigan wrote the definitive book in 1979 on the Sleeping Bear Dunes National Lakeshore legend entitled, Mishe Mokwa and the Legend of Sleeping Bear. A teacher and writer who began her graduate studies at the University of Arizona, she became entranced with legends and folklore during her undergraduate work at the University. During her years spent in Tucson and the Southwest, she began collecting Native American art, jewelry and legends, feeling an empathy with American Indian suffering.

Summers find Gloria at her Northern Michigan home surrounded by the lakes, rivers and forests of her birth. She winters in Tucson, Arizona and Hilton Head Island, South Carolina. This is her third book.